Boogly's fun with proverbs

Created and Written
By Grenville Solomon and Vinita Deshpande
Illustrated by Anne Angelshaug

Boogly is a painter robot. He lives in Robotic Park.

He paints beautiful pictures. All the robots love his pictures.

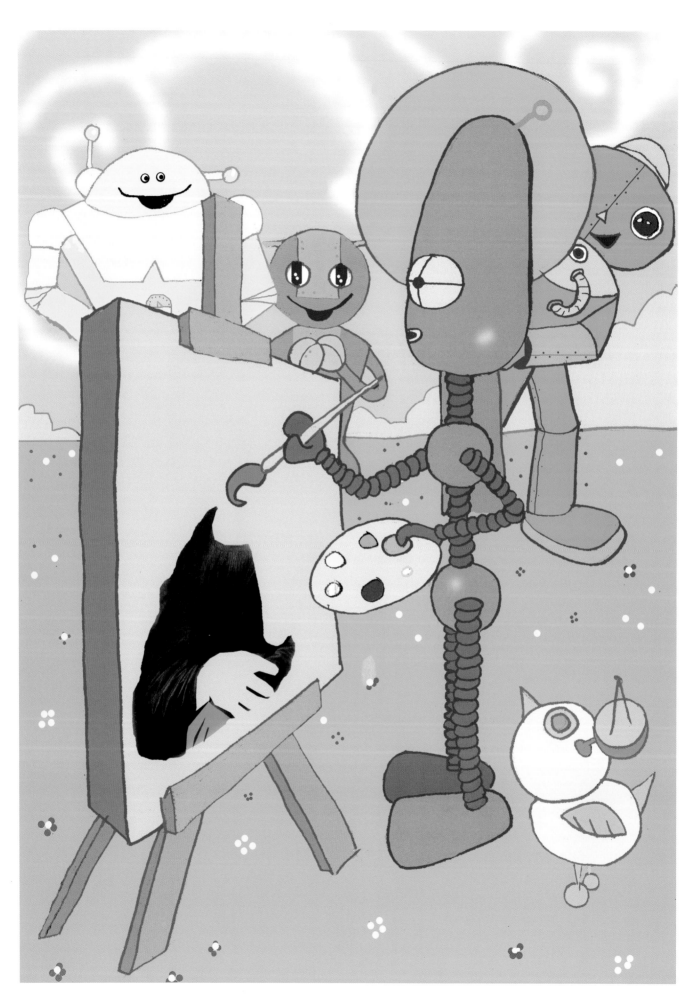

One day Boogly felt bored. He was tired of painting. He wanted to do something different. He thought to himself, "All the other robots are doing more interesting work. Why can't I do something different?"

He decided to read and learn new things. Robots read fast and remember everything they read. Boogly sat up late at night reading many new books.

He then went to the park manager, Mr Lee, and said, "I am bored with painting. I have read lots of books and have learnt many new things. I would like to do something different."

The park manager was worried. He thought Boogly was a good painter.

He was not sure whether Boogly should do something different. But he did not want to make Boogly feel sad.

He told Boogly, "I will give you three jobs. You will have to help the other robots do some tasks. If you succeed, then you can have the job you like."

First Boogly went to help Dakku, the cunning robot.

Dakku was always playing tricks and so he thought, "let's have some fun with Boogly." He told Boogly to cross a bridge. The bridge was broken in the centre.

Boogly walked to the centre of the bridge and scanned his memory. His data said "**Look before you leap**," which meant 'Be careful whilst crossing.' But Boogly was a learned robot now. He took the literal meaning of the proverb.

He understood this to mean, "look and then leap." And so he looked and then leapt, and fell bang through the centre of the bridge. Boogly was not too happy.

His next job was to help Goody the clever robot. He was busy fixing some light bulbs in the navigation room. Boogly was excited to help Goody fix bulbs.

He scanned his memory again. His data said, "**Many hands make light work,**" which meant 'two people can do the job faster than one.' "Wow that's simple," he thought to himself. He saw Goody standing on a ladder changing the light bulb and rushed up the ladder behind him.

Once again the learned Boogly took the literal meaning of the proverb. The more hands the better, he thought. He put both his hands on the bulb, and pushed with such force, that he broke the bulb and brought the ladder crashing down.

A disappointed Boogly went looking for Venda the strong robot, to try his hand at the third job. Venda was busy clearing the train tracks of some rocks that had fallen because of a landslide. He was lifting one rock at a time and putting it aside. Boogly thought, this is a difficult job and would take a long time.

However, he wanted to do it, so once again he scanned his memory. His data said, "**When you want to eat an elephant, eat one bite at a time.**" This meant, 'even difficult jobs can be done one step at a time.' Boogly was very confused. He was just wondering what to do when he saw an elephant crossing the road.

Boogly thought to himself, "Oh how silly! All I have to do is eat the elephant one bite at a time," and so he ran after the elephant. The poor elephant was so scared, that he ran for his life.

Boogly was very sad when he realised what he had done.
Mr. Lee came up to cheer him. He told Boogly, 'bookish
knowledge is not enough. You must learn how to use well
what you read.'

Boogly then went back to complete his painting.
After all, he was the best painter in Robotic Park.